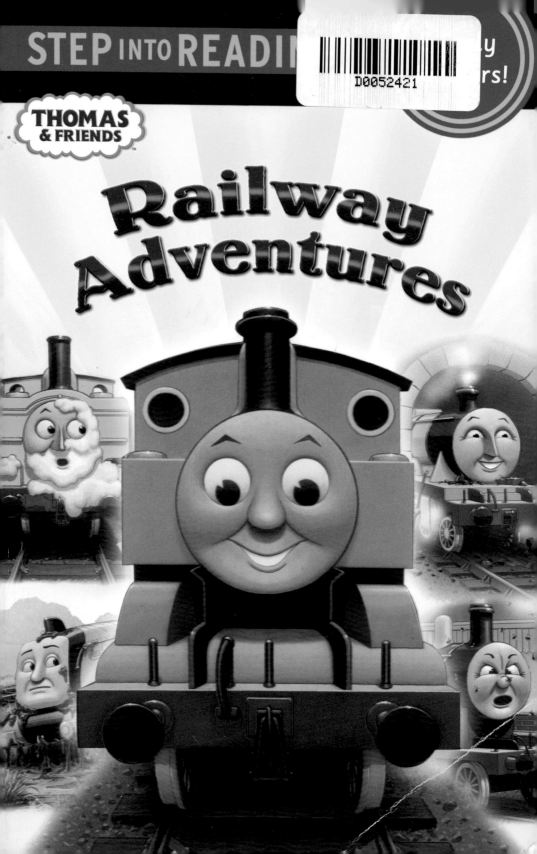

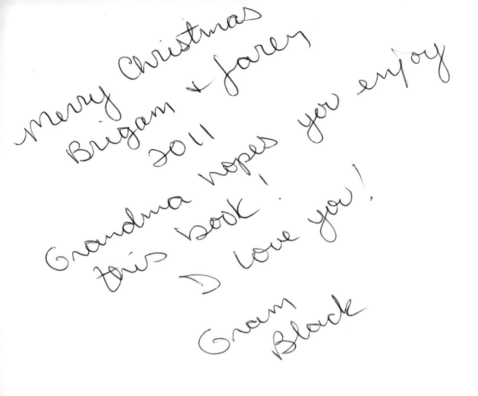

Merry Christmas
Brigam & Jarey
2011
Grandma hopes you enjoy
this book!
I love you!

Gram
Black

# Dear Parent:

Congratulations! Your child is taking the first steps on an exciting journey. The destination? Independent reading!

**STEP INTO READING®** will help your child get there. The program offers five steps to reading success. Each step includes fun stories and colorful art. There are also Step into Reading Sticker Books, Step into Reading Math Readers, Step into Reading Write-In Readers, Step into Reading Phonics Readers, and Step into Reading Phonics First Steps! Boxed Sets—a complete literacy program with something for every child.

## Learning to Read, Step by Step!

**Ready to Read   Preschool–Kindergarten**
• big type and easy words • rhyme and rhythm • picture clues
For children who know the alphabet and are eager to begin reading.

**Reading with Help   Preschool–Grade 1**
• basic vocabulary • short sentences • simple stories
For children who recognize familiar words and sound out new words with help.

**Reading on Your Own   Grades 1–3**
• engaging characters • easy-to-follow plots • popular topics
For children who are ready to read on their own.

**Reading Paragraphs   Grades 2–3**
• challenging vocabulary • short paragraphs • exciting stories
For newly independent readers who read simple sentences with confidence.

**Ready for Chapters   Grades 2–4**
• chapters • longer paragraphs • full-color art
For children who want to take the plunge into chapter books but still like colorful pictures.

**STEP INTO READING®** is designed to give every child a successful reading experience. The grade levels are only guides. Children can progress through the steps at their own speed, developing confidence in their reading, no matter what their grade.

Remember, a lifetime love of reading starts with a single step!

# Railway Adventures

Thomas the Tank Engine & Friends™

CREATED BY BRITT ALLCROFT

Based on The Railway Series by The Reverend W Awdry.
© 2010 Gullane (Thomas) LLC.
Thomas the Tank Engine & Friends and Thomas & Friends are trademarks of
Gullane (Thomas) Limited.
HIT and the HIT Entertainment logo are trademarks of HIT Entertainment Limited.

Step into Reading, Random House, and the Random House colophon are registered trademarks of
Random House, Inc.

Visit us on the Web!
www.stepintoreading.com
www.randomhouse.com/kids
www.thomasandfriends.com

Educators and librarians, for a variety of teaching tools, visit us at
www.randomhouse.com/teachers

*Library of Congress Cataloging-in-Publication Data*
Railway adventures / based on The railway series by The Reverend W. Awdry ;
illustrated by Richard Courtney.
   p. cm.
"Step 1 and Step 2 Books, A Collection of Five Early Readers."
"Thomas the Tank Engine & Friends"—Verso t.p.
Contents: Thomas and the jet engine—Stuck in the mud—The close shave—James goes buzz,
buzz—Henry and the elephant.
ISBN 978-0-375-86653-1
I. Courtney, Richard. II. Awdry, W. Railway series. III. Thomas the tank engine and friends.
PZ7.R1288 2010  [E]—dc22   2009034672

Printed in the United States of America
10 9 8 7 6 5 4 3

**THOMAS & FRIENDS™**

# Railway Adventures

Based on The Railway Series
by The Reverend W Awdry

Illustrated by Richard Courtney

Step 1 and Step 2 Books
A Collection of Five Early Readers

Random House New York

# Contents

THOMAS & FRIENDS™

# Thomas and the Jet Engine

Based on The Railway Series
by The Reverend W Awdry

Illustrated by Richard Courtney

Random House 🏠 New York

Thomas likes
to go fast.
Gordon thinks
he is faster.

Thomas must take
a jet engine
to the airport.

A jet engine goes
by pushing hot air
out its back.

It is like a balloon
full of air.

When you let it go,
off it zooms.

Cranky does not look.
His hook bumps
the switch.

# Click!

The jet engine
starts up!
Vroom! Vroom!

20

The jet engine rockets
Thomas up the track.

# Zoom! Zoom!

# Clear the lines!

# Runaway train!

Thomas passes Percy.

Whoosh!

Thomas passes Henry.

Whoosh!

Hi, Gordon!

Vroom!

Bye, Gordon!

Zoom!

At last,
the jet engine runs
out of fuel.
Phew!

Thomas chuffs
to the airport
on his own steam!

# Peep! Peep!

Back at the Shed,
Gordon ignores Thomas.
Humph!

Gordon may not be

a jet engine . . .

. . . but he <u>is</u>
full of hot air!

THOMAS & FRIENDS™

# Stuck in the Mud

Based on The Railway Series
by The Reverend W Awdry

Illustrated by Richard Courtney

Random House 🏠 New York

Click-clack!

Click-clack!

Thomas puffs
down the track.

# Thomas finds
# an old engine.

# Hiro is broken.

# Will he be sent
# to the scrap yard?

# No!

# Thomas will fix him.

# Uh-oh!

# Here comes Spencer!

# "I'm going to tell!"
## says Spencer.

Oh, no!

Hiro needs help!

# Thomas puffs off
# to get help.

# Click-clack!
# Click-clack!

Thomas and Spencer
race down the track.

# Splat!

# Spencer falls
# into the mud!

Now Thomas must help
<u>two</u> engines.

He tells Sir Topham Hatt.

Clang! Clang!

Bang! Bang!

Hiro is fixed.

But who will

help Spencer?

# Thomas is too small.

Hiro will.

He huffs and puffs.

He pulls Spencer
out of the mud.

"Thank you,"
says Spencer.

# Hooray for Hiro!

Click-clack!

Click-clack!

All the friends steam
down the track.

THOMAS & FRIENDS

# The Close Shave

Based on The Railway Series
by The Reverend W Awdry

Illustrated by Richard Courtney

Random House 🏠 New York

# Thomas and Duck
# are friends.

They are
not friends with the
Troublesome Trucks.

They like
to chug up hills.

They like
to zip down hills.

One day,
Duck was zipping
down a hill.
Hello, Thomas!

Duck heard

a warning whistle.

# "Peeeeeep! Peeeeeep!"

Trucks had run away
from Thomas.

# Go, Duck!

# No! Trucks!

# The Trucks
# bumped Duck.

# Mad Duck!

# Glad Trucks!

Duck and the Trucks
rushed down the hill.

Duck saw
the end of the line.
Duck had to stop!

Duck crashed
into the barber shop.

# Sad Duck!
# Bad Trucks!

The barber

was cross.

Soapy Duck.

# Dopey Trucks!

"I am sorry,"
said Duck.

"I had to stop
the runaway Trucks."

No one was hurt.

The shop could be fixed.

Duck was a hero!

Duck got cleaned up.

The Trucks
got picked up.

# Duck had
# a close shave!

STEP INTO READING®

STEP 2

THOMAS & FRIENDS™

# James Goes Buzz, Buzz

Based on The Railway Series
by The Reverend W Awdry

Illustrated by Richard Courtney

Random House 🏠 New York

It was a sunny day.

Chirp! Chirp!

sang the birds.

Buzz! Buzz!

hummed the bees.

Trevor the Tractor Engine
was hard at work.

Chug! Chug!
James pulled up.
"Hello, Trevor,"
said James.
"You look as busy
as a bee."

"I am!" said Trevor.

Buzz! Buzz!

"What is that noise?"

asked James.

"Bees," said Trevor.

"I am taking this beehive

to the station."

Buzz! Buzz!

buzzed the bees.

"Bees are very loud!"
said James.
"Do not make them mad,"
said Trevor.
"They may sting you!"

"Hmmmph!" said James.
"I am not scared of
a bunch of bees!"
James puffed off.

The next day,
James chugged into
the station.
He saw boxes
and bundles
and bags.
And there was
the beehive!

People rushed
this way and that.
BUMP!
A porter bumped
into the beehive!

The beehive broke!

Buzz! Buzz!

The bees buzzed

around the station.

Buzz! Buzz!
The bees buzzed
around James.
"Buzz buzz off!"
said James.
The bees
did not listen.

The bees buzzed onto
James' hot boiler.
One of the bees
burned his foot.
Buzz! Buzz! Buzz!
The bee was angry.

He stung James
on the nose!

"Eeeeeeeeeek,"
tooted James.
"Bad bee!"
James tried to make
the bees buzz off.

Chug! Chug!
James chugged
out of the station.

Whoosh!
He spun around
on the turntable.
Buzz! Buzz!
The bees liked the breeze.

Splash!

He tried to wash

them off.

Buzz! Buzz!

The bees took a bath.

Puff! Puff!

James blew smoke

at the bees.

Buzz! Buzz!

The bees did not budge.

James had an idea.

He turned around.

He chugged back
to find Trevor.

Buzz! Buzz!

The bees were home.

They buzzed back

into a beehive.

"Good bees!" said James.

"Goodbye, bees!"

## THOMAS & FRIENDS™

# Henry and the Elephant

Based on The Railway Series
by The Reverend W Awdry

Illustrated by Richard Courtney

Random House 🏠 New York

Thomas left the Yard.
He went to run
his own Branch Line.

Henry and Gordon

missed Thomas.

With Thomas gone,
there was more
work to do.
Henry and Gordon
were cross.

Henry grumbled
as he pushed trucks.
Gordon grumbled
as he pulled coaches.

One day,
a circus came
to town.

# Now the engines were even busier.

Henry pushed
the trucks.
Gordon pulled
the coaches.

They did not

grumble.

Henry and Gordon

liked the circus.

The next day,
Henry took workmen
to a blocked tunnel.

The workmen
picked up their tools.
"Time to clear the line."

They walked inside.

Something big was
in the tunnel.
It would not move.
It grunted.
It was alive!

# They ran outside.

The Foreman had a plan.
Henry could push trucks
into the tunnel.

"Wheesh," said Henry.
Henry did not like
tunnels.
He was scared.

Henry pushed the
trucks.
They went
into the dark tunnel.
BUMP!

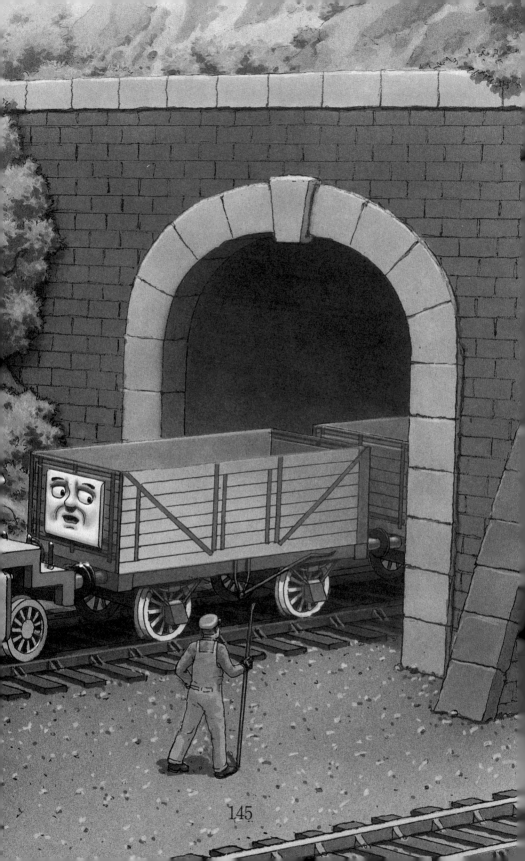

Henry pushed hard.
The big, scary thing
pushed back.

Henry pushed harder.
The big, scary thing
pushed hardest!
Henry inched
backwards.

First,
Henry was pushed
out of the tunnel.
Then the trucks
were pushed out.

At last,
they saw what
was in the tunnel.

It was an elephant!
And he looked cross.
He had run away
from the circus.

The workmen fed him
and gave him
lots of water.
The elephant felt better.